Magic Ballerina™

Rosa and the Special Prize

Darcey Bussell

HarperCollins *Children's Books*

Magic Ballerina
Rosa and the Special Prize

Welcome to the world of Enchantia!

I have always loved to dance. The captivating
music and wonderful stories of ballet are so
inspiring. So come with me and let's follow
Rosa on her magical adventures in
Enchantia, where the stories of dance will
take you on a very special journey.

p.s. Turn to the back to learn a special
dance step from me...

Special thanks to
Linda Chapman and
Nellie Ryan

First published in Great Britain by HarperCollins *Children's Books* 2009
HarperCollins *Children's Books* is a division of HarperCollins *Publishers* Ltd,
77-85 Fulham Palace Road, Hammersmith, London W6 8JB

The HarperCollins website address is
www.harpercollins.co.uk

1

Text copyright © HarperCollins *Children's Books* 2009
Illustrations by Nellie Ryan
Illustrations copyright © HarperCollins *Children's Books* 2009

MAGIC BALLERINA™ and the 'Magic Ballerina' logo are
trademarks of HarperCollins Publishers Ltd.

ISBN 978 0 00 785918 4

Printed and bound in England by
Clays Ltd, St Ives plc

To Phoebe and Zoe, as they are the inspiration behind Magic Ballerina.

Contents

Prologue

In the soft, pale light, the girl stood
with her head bent and her hands
held lightly in front of her.
There was a moment's silence and then the
first notes of the music began.
For as long as the girl could remember
music had seemed to tell her of
another world – a magical, exciting
world – that lay far, far away.
She always felt if she could just
close her eyes and lose herself,
then she would get there.
Maybe this time. As the music
swirled inside her, she swept
her arms above her head, rose on to
her toes and began to dance…

A Dream Come True

Rosa danced across the stage, turning with every step. Her pale blue ballet dress swirled around her as she stopped and spun on the spot. She was lost in the beautiful music, feeling like she really was a dancing water nymph. Ending her spin in a *demi-plié*, she held her arms up gracefully. The lights on stage were very bright and she couldn't see the faces in the audience, but she could hear the applause as it burst out!

She grinned and held out her hands to the sides. The other girls on the stage ran forward and made a line with her. They were all dressed in different shades of green and blue. They curtseyed together, smiling happily, and then the curtains closed.

Rosa's best friend, Olivia, hugged her. "Wasn't that brilliant?"

Rosa's eyes shone. "It was!" Her class had been performing a ballet at the local theatre about an underwater kingdom and she had been the main character, a water nymph called Ondine.

"Come on, girls!" Madame Za-Za, their teacher, called from the side of the stage. "Off you come!"

As they left through the wings, Madame Za-Za smiled warmly at them. "That was excellent, all of you!" She turned to smile at Rosa in particular. "Well done. I don't think you have ever danced so well, Rosa."

Rosa glowed with pride as she went downstairs to the dressing rooms with Olivia. There was a TV monitor on the wall which showed what was happening on stage.

The next class were performing the Sugar Plum Fairy's dance from *The Nutcracker*. Rosa glanced at her red ballet shoes and smiled to herself. It was amazing to think that she had actually met the *real* Sugar Plum Fairy...

Rosa had a secret. Her red ballet shoes were magic! Sometimes they started to sparkle and then they took her to Enchantia, a land where all the different characters from the ballets lived. Rosa had been on some

brilliant adventures there. She wondered
when she'd go again.

"Hey, Rosa! Have some of these!"

Looking round, Rosa saw that her friends
were sharing out a big bag of sweets. Pushing
the thoughts of Enchantia away, she ran over
to join them.

After the show, the girls piled out of the
dressing rooms and into the theatre foyer
to meet their parents. They were all
chattering excitedly. Madame Za-Za had
given them each a glittering hairslide as an
after-show present. Rosa's was made of
sparkling red jewels and she had clipped it
into her blonde hair.

"There's my mum and dad," said Olivia. "See you tomorrow, Rosa."

She ran off. Rosa caught sight of her own mum. She was talking to a slim auburn-haired lady who had a notepad in her hands.

"Mum!" Rosa called.

Rosa's mother looked around and her face lit up with a proud smile. "You were wonderful, sweetheart," she said as Rosa hurried over.

Rosa grinned happily. Her mum had been a fantastic ballet dancer before a car accident had left her in a wheelchair. Rosa's dream was to be a ballerina just like her one day.

"Rosa, this is Imogen Green," her mum went on. "We used to dance together when we were younger, but now she works for the Royal Ballet School."

Rosa's eyes widened as she looked at the red-haired lady. The Royal Ballet School! That was where her mum had trained. Everyone knew it was the best ballet school in the country.

"Hello, Rosa." Imogen smiled at her. "My job is to help organise the auditions for the Royal Ballet School. I am a friend of Madame Za-Za's and she told me she had some very talented young dancers in her classes. Would you be interested in auditioning?"

"Oh, yes!" Rosa exclaimed in delight.

"I have a list of other girls here too," said Imogen, looking down at her notepad. "There was a girl called Olivia in your class and a few girls from the class above."

Oh, wow! Rosa's head spun. She couldn't wait to tell everyone!

"Obviously this is just an audition and there's no guarantee that you would get a place at the school," Imogen went on.

"And if you did it's a big decision because it would mean coming to live in London and attending boarding school."

Boarding school! Rosa felt as if a bucket of water had just been dumped over her.

She couldn't do that. It was just her and her mum because her dad wasn't around any more. She couldn't leave her mum on her own to go to boarding school. She stared at Imogen in dismay.

"Rosa?" her mum said, catching her expression. "Is something wrong?"

"I... I hadn't realised it would be boarding!" stammered Rosa.

"Don't you want to board?" her mum asked in surprise.

Rosa hesitated. *If I say I don't want to go because it will leave Mum on her own, she'll feel really guilty.* "I... um... no, not really," she lied.

Imogen nodded understandingly. "Some girls do find the idea of boarding very difficult. And maybe you'll find that the Royal Ballet School isn't right for you, Rosa. But why don't you have a think about it?

I've given the forms to your mum. If you do decide to audition you need to send them off in the next few days." She smiled. "Now, I'd better go and speak to the others. Maybe I'll see you again soon." She hurried off.

Rosa swallowed. The thought of being able to dance every day, living with other girls who were mad about ballet too, taking lots and lots of different dancing classes... It sounded like heaven! But what about her mum? She couldn't leave her, could she?

Rosa's mother squeezed her hand. "Don't look so anxious, sweetheart. I thought you'd leap at the chance of auditioning, but of course you don't have to try for a place if you don't really want to."

But I do want to!

Rosa bit the words back.

"We'll talk about it when we get home," her mum said.

Rosa nodded sadly, but inside she knew there was nothing to talk about. How *could* she go? She just couldn't!

Sparkling Shoes!

"What do you mean, you're not going to audition?" Olivia sounded shocked. Rosa had only been home about ten minutes when the phone had rung. It had been her best friend, bubbling with excitement at the news. "You have to go! Oh, just imagine if we both got in, Rosa. It would be so cool! And I heard Delphie, Lola and

Sukie have all been asked to audition too!"

Rosa didn't say anything. The thought of the others from Madame Za-Za's school going to the auditions, maybe getting in, and going to the Royal Ballet School without her, made her want to cry. And if Olivia went she wouldn't even have a best friend at Madame Za-Za's any more.

"You just have to audition," Olivia told her.

"I can't!" Rosa burst out. "Because…"

Just then her mum came into the lounge where Rosa was talking. "Because I don't want to," Rosa said quickly.

"But why?" Olivia sounded completely confused.

"I just don't." Rosa felt tears starting to prickle in her eyes. "Look, I've got to go," she said, knowing that if she didn't get off the phone straight away she might really start to cry. "I'll see you tomorrow."

She pressed the off button on the phone.

"Rosa, can we talk about the auditions?" her mum said gently. "There's something the matter, I know there is. I can't believe you don't want to go."

Rosa looked at her. "You don't want me to go to the Royal Ballet School, do you, Mum? You don't want me to board and be away from you?"

"Well, I don't *want* you to but…"

"Well, then that's OK," Rosa interrupted. She could hear that her voice sounded higher than normal. "Because I don't want to go either." She forced herself to smile. "I'm fine about it, Mum, really. I'm not going to audition. I'm just going to my bedroom for a bit."

She ran out of the lounge and along the corridor to her room. Her mum had left the leaflet about the auditions on her bed, together with her dancing clothes and red ballet shoes. Rosa slowly went over.

Longing shot through her as she looked at the application form.

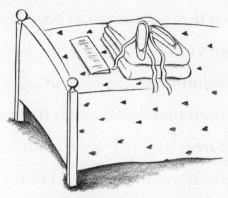

I want to go so much, she thought. *I want to audition and that lady thought I was good enough.*

She reached for her ballet shoes. Whenever she was feeling really happy or really sad, she always danced. Her feet seemed to want to turn her feelings into ballet steps. She put the shoes on and, hearing the music from the show in her head, she started to dance around her bedroom. Moving forward with tiny steps, she swayed her arms one way and then the other. Her feet started to tingle…

Glancing down, she saw that her ballet shoes were sparkling. *Oh, wow! I'm going to Enchantia again*, she thought.

A swirling haze of green, blue and silvery light surrounded her and she was lifted into the air. Her unhappiness about the auditions vanished at the thought of seeing all her friends in Enchantia again. *What adventure am I going to have this time?* she wondered excitedly.

As the magic set her gently down, she could hear the sound of seagulls crying and of waves breaking on a beach. The silvery light cleared and Rosa saw that she was by the sea. There were rocky cliffs in front of her with jagged sides and cave openings. The waves were stormy and grey, and a cold wind was whipping through her hair. Rosa shivered and looked around. She'd never been in this part of Enchantia before. Why had the magic brought her here?

"Rosa!"

Rosa looked around to see her friend, Nutmeg, the fairy of the spices, standing at the top of the cliff, being blown about by the gusts of wind. She was dressed in a pale pink and brown tutu.

"Hi, Nutmeg!" Rosa called.

The fairy came scrambling down the cliff.
She reached the bottom and ran over.
"Oh, this wind, it's
so strong!" She
hugged Rosa.
"I'm very glad
you've come,
Rosa."

"It's freezing
here!" said Rosa,
hugging her back.

Nutmeg nodded.
"There's stormy
weather all the time at the moment –
it's because King Tristan has fallen out
with King Neptune." Rain started to fall

and there was a deep rumble of thunder.

"Quick! Let's go into one of the caves and I'll tell you the whole story. We'll get soaked if we stay out here."

Rosa ran after Nutmeg to the nearest cave in the cliffs, thinking hard. She knew King Tristan was the King of Enchantia – she had met him on her previous adventures – but who was King Neptune? She didn't have time to dwell on it for long as Nutmeg had started to whisper.

"Try not to make too much noise when we get inside!" the fairy said anxiously. "Cave sprites live in the hollows of these cliffs."

"Cave sprites?" Rosa echoed, her ballet shoes slipping on the damp rock. "What are they?"

33

"They're really naughty, vain creatures," said Nutmeg. "They love playing tricks and annoying people. If you go into their caves and they find you, they always poke you and pinch you, and chase you out."

Rosa didn't like the sound of them at all!

They reached the cave. Rosa looked round anxiously, wondering if she would see a cave sprite, but it was empty.

"So what's been going on?" she said in a low voice.

Nutmeg rubbed her bare arms. "I'll help us to get warm and then I'll explain…"

A Song In the Cave

Nutmeg waved her wand and conjured up
two thick fur-lined coats. Rosa pulled one
thankfully around herself, covering up her
damp jeans and T-shirt. "I'd magic up a
fire, but it might make a sprite come,"
Nutmeg whispered. "But we can have
these to eat." She waved her wand again.
With a tinkle of music, two currant buns

appeared on her lap. She handed one to
Rosa. It was warm and smelt sweet, and
slightly spicy.

"Thank you!"

As Rosa bit into the delicious bun she felt a
bit better. She looked at the fairy who was
huddling into her coat. "So what's been
happening, Nutmeg?"

"Well, all this stormy weather is because
two kings have fallen out. They're cousins,"
Nutmeg explained. "You know King Tristan
of course – the king of the land. Well, King
Neptune is king of the sea in Enchantia. They
haven't got on since they had a fencing
competition over a beautiful jewelled sceptre
that belonged to their grandfather. King
Neptune won and took the special prize to his

underwater kingdom. Then a few days ago, the sceptre was stolen! King Neptune was so angry, he sent storms all over the land. Everyone is really miserable because it's too windy to dance outside and the thunder drowns out any music inside, so we can't dance anywhere! King Neptune says he won't stop the storms until King Tristan gives him the sceptre back."

"Well, why doesn't King Tristan just give it back?" asked Rosa.

"Because he hasn't got it," said Nutmeg. "King Tristan didn't take it. He's got

absolutely no idea where it is, but King
Neptune is refusing to talk to him. If only
they'd just listen to each other, maybe they'd
be able to sort this out, but they won't. The
only way to stop the storms is to find the
sceptre and give it back. Everyone's
been looking and no one has found it yet."
She pulled her coat around her miserably.
"I don't know what we're going to do."

Rosa wracked her brains. If no one even
knew who had taken the sceptre, how
could they possibly try and get it back?
It seemed impossible. Suddenly she heard
a high-pitched voice singing a song:

"Made of brightest, purest gold
and wanted by the king…

He thinks his cousin stole it – ha!

He doesn't know a thing…"

"What's that?" whispered Rosa in surprise.
The voice seemed to be coming from a tunnel
at the back of the cave.

"It's a cave sprite!" hissed Nutmeg. "Be really quiet."

Rosa frowned. "But listen to the words he's singing, Nutmeg."

> *"Cos I took it, yes I did.*
> *I swam and got it, oh, I did,*
> *And now there's lots of storms,*
> *cos the thing's been hid!"*

Rosa turned to Nutmeg. "It sounds like he's singing about the sceptre!" Her voice rose in excitement. "It sounds like he took it!"

"Sssh, Rosa!" Nutmeg hushed quickly.

But Rosa had jumped to her feet. "Hey!" she called loudly, interrupting the song. "Hey, whoever's singing! Come out and talk to us!"

"Rosa!" Nutmeg gasped. "What are you doing?"

The singing stopped abruptly. Rosa held her breath. What was going to happen? There was a scrabbling of feet and suddenly a bony sprite burst out of the tunnel at the back of the cave. He had long spindly arms and legs, a hooked nose, and a few thin tufts of hair that fell forward over his eyes.

He was wearing raggedy brown trousers
and was about the same size as Rosa.

"People! Here!" He launched himself
at Rosa, his long bony fingers poking her.
"Ha! So you thought you'd come into
Solly the sprite's cave, did you, little girl?
And who's this? A silly fairy in a tutu!" He
started pinching Nutmeg, whirling round
her as he did so. She squealed as he cackled

with laughter. "Out, out, out, out, OUT!" he cried. "Solly doesn't like visitors!"

Nutmeg pushed past him and ran to the cave entrance.

The sprite dashed over to Rosa, leaping into the air, all bony arms and legs. He landed nimbly and pulled her hair.

"Ow! Stop it!" she exclaimed.

"Go on! Go, go, go, go!" he cried, poking her in the ribs and spinning round again, his hair flopping over his face. "This is Solly's cave, this is!"

But Rosa stood firm. "I won't go! I want to know about the sceptre!"

The sprite stopped instantly and a cunning look came into his small dark eyes. "The sceptre? Ooooh, I don't know anything about that." He shook his head vigorously. "Oh, no, Solly the sprite doesn't know anything at all, not a single itty-bitty thing."

"But you were singing about it!" Rosa said.

The sprite folded his bony arms. "Just a song. A sprite can sing. Solly likes to sing."

Rosa didn't believe him for a second.

"You do know something about it!"

The sprite shook his head. "Don't!"

"You do!"

"Don't!"

Rosa stared at him and then suddenly she remembered what Nutmeg had said about cave sprites being vain. *Maybe...* She sighed dramatically. "Oh well. I must be wrong, then. You know, I thought you must have been the person who had taken the sceptre, because only someone who was very clever could have stolen it. But I guess you're not that clever after all. It must have been someone else. I'm sorry to have bothered you." She started walking towards Nutmeg at the entrance to the cave.

"Wait!" the sprite jumped in front of her.

Rosa stopped and turned around, and Nutmeg moved to her side.

"All right, maybe…" he said slowly. "Just maybe, it *was* clever, sly Solly."

"Well, was it?" Rosa asked eagerly.

The sprite hesitated and then the words burst out of him. "Oh, yes, all right. It was!" he said, dancing round, looking suddenly proud. "Solly the sprite did it! Solly swam down under the sea and waited until silly Neptune and all his mer-people went hunting for fish, and then Solly snatched it! Ha!"

"But why?" asked Nutmeg.

Solly chuckled gleefully. "Cos it made Neptune cross. Silly old king with his silly old sceptre! Solly likes making people cross."

"But now there's lots of storms all across Enchantia," said Nutmeg.

"Good!" The sprite cackled. "Solly hid it

and now Neptune can't find it!"

"Where did you hide it?" Rosa asked quickly.

Solly looked crafty. "Not telling."

"Oh, please," Rosa begged. "I bet it was a very clever place."

'No, no, no, no, no! Solly isn't going to say a thing!"

Rosa felt a wave of frustration as she looked at the sprite shaking his head. If he wasn't going to tell them, what were they going to do now?

Ballet Magic!

Rosa pushed her hands through her hair in exasperation. Her new hairslide fell out and clattered to the floor where it glittered in the dim light.

"What's that?' demanded the sprite.

"My hairslide," Rosa replied, picking it up.

"Hair…slide," Solly repeated the word slowly as if he'd never heard it before. He

reached up and touched his long, floppy fringe thoughtfully, then he looked at her. "Solly wants it."

Rosa stared at him. "No."

"Give it to Solly, little girl," he wheedled. "Solly needs it."

"No way!" Rosa replied. "It's mine and it's new. Anyway, why would I give it to you?" She broke off and looked at him, an idea popping into her head. "Unless… Yes! You can have the hairslide if you tell me where the sceptre is."

Solly looked at the slide and then looked at her. He seemed to be thinking it over.

Rosa held her breath. Would he tell them? She loved the slide, but she wanted to help Nutmeg and everyone else in Enchantia more. She turned it so that the jewels caught the light. "Look at it. It's lovely and sparkly, and ever so useful," she said temptingly.

The sprite hesitated and then nodded, making his hair fall over his eyes again. "All right, Solly'll tell you!" he said, his eyes gleaming. "Solly hid the sceptre in the Great Green Cave!" He snatched the hairslide.

In an instant, Rosa's hairslide was gone, but instead of feeling upset, she just felt a rush of triumph. *Yes!* Now they knew where the sceptre was, they could go and get it. Nutmeg's magic could take them anywhere in Enchantia, so it should be easy!

The sprite clipped the slide into his hair. It looked very strange, but he seemed pleased.

Pulling a mirror from his trouser pocket, he admired himself. "Who's a good-looking sprite, then?" he preened. "Ooooh, yes, Solly, you're a proper handsome one." He looked at Rosa and chuckled. "And proper clever too…" He started to sing again.

"The slide's a delight
Says Solly the sprite!
It looks such a treat in his hair

But the sceptre you seek
can't be reached by the weak,
or by humans who need to
breathe air!"

Rosa and Nutmeg stared at him. "What do you mean? You said it was in a cave!" exclaimed Rosa.

"And so it is," cackled Solly. "But…" He burst into song again:

"The cave's full of seaweed,
green, gold and brown,
and if you try to get there,
you'll certainly DROWN!"

Nutmeg gasped. "The cave's underwater!"

"Deep, deep down under the waves." The sprite danced around gleefully. "Tricked you! Tricked you! You thought you'd be able to get it, but you can't!" He started to poke and pinch them again.

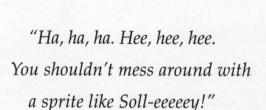

"Ha, ha, ha. Hee, hee, hee.
You shouldn't mess around with
a sprite like Soll-eeeeey!"

Rosa and Nutmeg stumbled out of the cave and on to the beach. The storm had passed and the rain had stopped, but the sea still looked wild and the grey clouds were pressing down on the land and water.

"What are we going to do, Rosa?" said Nutmeg in dismay. "He's right, we can't go down into the sea."

Rosa stared out at the waves crashing on to the beach. "But we can't give up." She thought about the ballet she'd been dancing at home. " Oh, I wish I was a water nymph and could breathe underwater."

Nutmeg caught her breath. "Oh!"

Rosa looked at her.

"What?"

"I think I might just have had an idea! If we dance like water nymphs really, really well – so well that we almost become them – then the magic of the ballet will help us. It'll make us become like water nymphs and we'll be able to breathe underwater. The magic won't last forever, but for a little while we'll be able to go under the waves."

"So we could swim down and see if we can find this cave?" asked Rosa eagerly.

Nutmeg nodded.

Rosa flung off her heavy coat. "Then let's do it!"

The two of them hurried down to the beach. Nutmeg waved her wand and music flooded out. It was the same music that

Rosa had danced to at the performance that afternoon. As they spun across the sand, lost in the music, Rosa felt her whole body starting to tingle. She looked down and gasped. Her skin was suddenly sparkling with tiny water droplets and her clothes had changed into a knee-length silvery-green dress.

"The magic's working!" Nutmeg exclaimed. "Quick, Rosa! We'll be able to go underwater now! But be careful. There are some dangerous creatures in the sea, like poisonous jellyfish, serpents and sea dragons, not to mention King Neptune himself. He's not usually very friendly to people from the land. Keep a look out!"

She ran towards the sea. Rosa's heart

thumped. The water looked very cold, but Nutmeg jumped straight in! Screwing up her face for courage, Rosa plunged into the waves expecting the water to be icy, but to her astonishment it was as warm as a bath now that the magic was protecting her.

Rosa dived under the waves after Nutmeg and swam down and down…

Hide and Seek

As Rosa and Nutmeg swam towards the
ocean floor, multi-coloured shoals of fish
came swooping around them. There were
twisted rock formations, massive clumps
of seaweed and carpets of pink anemones
waving their tentacles. A faint watery
music seemed to echo in their ears.

"What's that?" Rosa asked curiously.

"It's the song of the sea," Nutmeg replied. "The music that all the sea creatures can dance to if they want." As Rosa watched a shoal of green and yellow fish dive and swoop together, she realised it did almost look as if they were dancing.

"Careful!" Nutmeg suddenly grabbed Rosa's arm and pulled her to one side. A large black and yellow striped jellyfish had come bobbing out from behind a rock, its long tentacles trailing.

"That's a really poisonous type of jellyfish," Nutmeg explained. "Don't go near it."

Rosa swam quickly out of its way. It was amazing being under the sea even though there were dangerous creatures to avoid.

"Where's the Great Green Cave? Can you use your magic to take us there, Nutmeg?"

"No, my magic won't work underwater," Nutmeg replied. "Let's ask those fish over there if they know where it is." She swam towards a shoal of tiny blue fish. "Excuse me…"

But the fish raced away in a glowing cloud.

Rosa heard a giggle. She turned and saw someone duck behind a rock – it was a girl in a silvery dress.

Nutmeg hadn't noticed. "Maybe I'll ask that octopus," she was saying, heading over to a large creature who was swimming along by the ocean floor. But as soon as she spoke to him, he shot away in a cloud of bubbles.

"Why won't anyone help?" exclaimed Nutmeg in frustration.

Rosa was still staring at the rock. Was someone really there? She swam over. There was another giggle behind her. She looked round and caught sight of the same girl, diving gracefully behind a large blue sea sponge.

"Hey!" Rosa called. "Come here!" She swam to the sponge, but when she got there, the girl had gone. "I saw someone," Rosa said, going back to Nutmeg.

Two clumps of seaweed suddenly dropped on to their heads. They looked up to see a girl swimming above them; she had wavy blonde hair and an impish face. She put her tongue out, twirled round and then dashed away giggling.

"It's a water nymph!" exclaimed Nutmeg.

"They're like mermaids, but they have legs not a tail and they can go out on to the beach as well as living in the sea."

"Wait!" called Rosa. "Please will you help us?"

Rosa and Nutmeg chased after the nymph, but she was a much faster swimmer than them and swam around a clump of seaweed. When Rosa and Nutmeg reached it, she'd gone.

Rosa bit her lip. She was beginning to feel that they were never going to find the Great Green Cave. No one seemed to want to help them and she wasn't sure how long their magic would last.

Suddenly there was a high-pitched scream from a cluster of tall rocks just ahead. "What was that?" Rosa said in alarm.

"Help!" a frightened voice cried.

Rosa and Nutmeg swam to the rocks as quickly as they could.

The sight there made Rosa's eyes widen. The water nymph was standing in a crack between two of the rocks from which she had been spying on Rosa and Nutmeg, but one of the poisonous black and yellow jellyfish had floated after her and was now blocking the entrance. She was trapped!

She saw Rosa and Nutmeg looking at her. "Help me! Please!" she gasped in terror. "He's going to sting me!"

Rosa grabbed a handful of shells from the ocean floor and threw them at the jellyfish but it just made him bob closer to the terrified nymph.

The nymph started to cry.

"What can we do?" Rosa asked Nutmeg frantically.

"I know!" Nutmeg exclaimed. "I bet he doesn't like nutmeg!" She swam up, hovered in the water above the jellyfish and waved her wand. Brown spicy nutmeg powder sprinkled out and fell on the jellyfish. A shiver ran through its gloomy body. Nutmeg waved her wand harder. A whole load more nutmeg fell out! The jellyfish's sides started to puff out…

"What's happening to it?" Rosa said.

Suddenly, the jellyfish sneezed!

Rosa only just managed to jump out of the way in time as the force of the sneeze sent the jellyfish shooting backwards away from the crack in the rocks. The water nymph dashed out after him.

"Oh, thank you! Thank you!" she cried in relief as the jellyfish bobbed away looking confused. "You rescued me!"

"I wasn't sure if nutmeg would work, but

I'm glad it did!" Nutmeg smiled at her. "What's your name?"

"Alina," the nymph replied. "What's yours and what are you doing here?"

Rosa quickly told Alina their names and explained. "So, you see we have to find the Great Green Cave," she finished.

"Oh, I know where that is!" said Alina.

"Could you tell us how to get there?" asked Rosa eagerly.

Alina grinned. "I'll do better than that. I'll take you there! Come on!"

The Great Green Cave

Rosa and Nutmeg raced after the water nymph. Alina was so fast, she had to keep stopping and waiting for them to catch up.

"Are we nearly there?" said Nutmeg after they had been swimming for some time. Her face was pale and she was breathing heavily. "I'm not sure my ballet magic is going to last much longer."

Rosa realised that she too was feeling out of breath. "How much further is it?" she asked anxiously.

"We'll be there soon," Alina said.

As they swam on, Rosa felt her breath getting shorter and shorter. Just when she was beginning to think she couldn't go on any further, Alina stopped. "There it is!" She pointed to a cave in front of them. A curtain of thick green seaweed hung down over the entrance. "That's the Great Green Cave!"

Rosa's ears were drumming and her chest was really hurting now. She was horribly aware she was deep under the sea and the magic could run out at any second. She just wanted to get to the surface. Turning, she saw Nutmeg leaning against a rock, panting for breath.

I've got to get the sceptre, Rosa thought. She swam as quickly as she could into the cave and looked around. It was full of brown and green seaweed. *But where was King Neptune's sceptre?* Rosa looked around desperately.

And then she saw it! A tall, thin pole with a jewel-encrusted ball at the top was poking out from a thick clump of rubbery brown weed. Rosa's heart jumped. Using the last of her fading strength, she swam over and pulled the sceptre out. "I've got it!" she gasped as she left the cave.

"Brilliant," Nutmeg panted. "Let's get back to the surface now! I can hardly breathe."

"I hope we've got enough magic to get there," said Rosa.

"I'll help!" Alina grabbed their hands and started to pull them upwards. With her strength and both of them kicking frantically, Rosa and  Nutmeg got closer and closer to the surface. Just when Rosa felt she had run out of her very last breath, they burst out into the air.

"We did it!" Nutmeg cried in relief as the grey waves rolled around them.

Rosa drew in deep gulps of fresh air. They were the sweetest breaths she had ever taken. She clutched the sceptre, trying to hang on to it and swim at the same time.

"The beach is a long way away," she realised anxiously.

"Don't worry, now we're not underwater, I can use my magic to get us there," said Nutmeg. "Do you want to come with us, Alina?"

"Could I really? I've never travelled by fairy magic before," said the nymph shyly.

Nutmeg grinned. "Of course you can!"

Pulling out her wand, she twirled around

in the water. A cloud of silver sparkles surrounded them. Nutmeg grabbed Rosa and Alina's hands, and the next minute they were spinning round and lifting into the air. Her magic put them down again on the beach at the edge of the waves.

"Phew!" Rosa said.

"That was fun!" said Alina in delight.

"Thank you so much for helping us," Rosa said to her. "We'd never have got this sceptre back without you. Now we have to work out how to get it back to King Neptune..."

There was an enormous crash of thunder and suddenly something erupted through the waves. Rosa stared. It was a very large man standing astride the back of two dolphins. He had strong white hair and was holding a trident in his hand – a massive fork with three sharp prongs – and as he stopped on the surface of the water, three seagulls flew down to perch on his massive shoulders.

"King Neptune!" Alina gasped.

A familiar bony head with a tuft of hair
held back by a red slide surfaced in the water
beside the dolphins. "It was her!" shrieked
Solly the sprite, pointing a long bony arm at
Rosa. "That's the human girl Solly was
telling you about, your majesty. That's the
one who stole your sceptre. Clever old Solly
the Sprite told you, yes he did!"

"YOU!" the sea king thundered, his eyes
on Rosa.

"Me? I didn't steal it!" gasped Rosa.

The king didn't listen to her. "Thief!" he roared.

"But it wasn't Rosa, King Neptune!" Nutmeg cried. "It was…"

"It was that girl!" shrieked the sprite. "Solly heard her plotting it in his cave. Solly swam all the way out to your kingdom to tell you, your majesty. Ooooh, Solly deserves a proper reward for his bravery, he does."

"He's lying!" Alina cried.

But Neptune didn't listen to her either. "And I thought it was my cousin who had wronged me by taking it, when all along it was you, human girl!" He raised his trident and pointed it straight at Rosa. "Well, I will have my revenge! You shall be punished!"

Neptune's Revenge

Rosa's heart pounded. If only she could make Neptune stop and listen, so they could explain the truth. But how could she manage that? She did the only thing that came into her head – she danced! Hearing the music in her mind, she danced like a water nymph again. The sand by the water was firm and damp, and she spun across it with light steps, her arms moving like seaweed in the water.

"Good idea, Rosa!" she heard Nutmeg cry. There was a tinkle of Nutmeg's wand and real music flooded out. Rosa lost herself in it, turning round faster and faster.

As she paused for a moment on her toes, with her arms above her head, she dared to glance at King Neptune. He was staring straight at her.

"You dance like a nymph from the water!" his voice rumbled in astonishment. "How can that be?"

Rosa seized her chance. Running forward she placed the sceptre at the water's edge and swept into a deep curtsey. "King Neptune, here's your sceptre. I promise I didn't steal it. I was trying to find it with Nutmeg because we wanted you to stop the storms. Here. Please, have it back!"

"Don't listen to her!" shrieked Solly.

"Please do listen, your majesty!" Alina exclaimed. She picked the sceptre up and swam to the king, holding it out. "It's the truth. Rosa and Nutmeg have been trying to get the sceptre back for you. They had to be very brave and go far under the water to do it, because it was hidden in the Great Green Cave. I helped them find the way there. Rosa really didn't steal the sceptre from you."

"So who did?" the sea king demanded, bending down and taking the sceptre from the nymph.

Rosa hesitated, but Alina and Nutmeg had no such scruples. "He did!" they both said, turning and pointing at Solly.

"Solly? Oh, no, no, no," said the sprite hastily, starting to swim backwards away from the king.

"Is this true, sprite?" Neptune demanded as Alina joined Rosa and Nutmeg again.

"No, of course not! No, it wasn't Solly, no," the cave sprite blustered.

"He did do it! He did it just to cause mischief!" said Nutmeg. "He told us!"

Neptune looked from the girls to the sprite. "Bah! I should have known better than to believe a tricky cave sprite!" he roared. He pointed at Solly. "See him off!" he shouted to the seagulls.

The birds instantly swooped down on to the sprite, pecking and prodding him with their beaks.

"Ow! Ooh! Ah! Ow!" Solly swam towards the shore as fast as he could. Reaching the beach, he scrambled out of the water. The slide fell out of his hair, but he didn't have time to get it. Racing away up the beach, he was chased all the way back to his cave by the gulls.

"And may that be a lesson to you, sprite!" Neptune thundered after him.

Alina picked up the hairslide and held it out to Rosa. "What's this? It's very pretty."

"It's a hairslide. It was mine." Rosa made a quick decision. "But you can have it now, Alina." She wanted to say thank you. "We'd never have found the cave without you."

"It's beautiful!" Alina said in delight. She clipped it into her wavy hair. "Thank you!"

Neptune held up his sceptre. "My special prize," he said lovingly. "I should have listened to my cousin. I have been punishing him unfairly. To make amends, I will stop these storms and make it the most perfect day that Enchantia has ever seen." Raising his trident to the sky, he called out a deep command in a language that Rosa didn't understand.

The clouds above seemed to shiver and then they split apart, racing away to leave behind a pale blue sky. The wind dropped and the waves instantly calmed. As the sun sparkled on the rock pools, Rosa felt her spirits soar.

Nutmeg waved her wand and the watery music started up again. The fairy grabbed Rosa and Alina's hands and swung them round.

We did it! Rosa thought. *We got the sceptre back. The storms have gone!*

The seagulls swooped through the air and a shoal of flying fish leapt out of the waves as if they were dancing too.

"Goodbye, human girl and fairy!" called King Neptune. "Take these gifts as a reward for so bravely returning my sceptre." He threw two beautiful pink and cream curly shells into the air and they flew across the waves. "May they always sing to you with the voice of the sea and remind you of your adventures in my kingdom."

Rosa and Nutmeg caught the shells.

"Thank you!" they cried as Neptune and his dolphins sank down beneath the waves.

"Oh, wait until we get back to the Royal Palace and tell the King and Queen about all of this!" said Nutmeg, skipping in delight. "They are going to be so pleased!"

But just as she spoke, Rosa's ballet shoes started to sparkle. "I can't go to the palace! I'm going home!" cried Rosa. "Bye, Nutmeg! Bye, Alina!"

As her friends called goodbye, the world blurred into a swirl of colours and suddenly she was swept away...

Coming Home

Rosa landed in her bedroom and blinked.
It was always strange coming back to real
life after having been in Enchantia. Realising
she had the shell, in her hands, she lifted
it to her ear. It made the sound of the waves
just like a normal shell, but as well as the
swirling whooshing sound, there was a
faint tinkling of beautiful watery music.

Rosa smiled. Neptune was right. The shell would always remind her of the adventure under the sea. She put it down on her bedside table. As she did so, her eyes fell on the Royal Ballet School forms form on her bed. Of course, the auditions! Everything came rushing back. She picked up the leaflet and looked at it sadly.

Just then there was a sound behind her. Rosa turned and saw her mum in the doorway. "Rosa, can we talk? I really want to know why you don't want to go to the auditions." Her mum wheeled herself into the room. "It just seems so unlike you. Are you telling me the truth?"

Rosa thought about her adventure in Enchantia. So much trouble had been caused by King Neptune refusing to talk to King Tristan. She felt awkward about it, but she suddenly knew she should be honest with her mum.

"Actually, I… I do want to go to the auditions," she admitted. "And I do want to go to the Royal Ballet School, it's just… just…" The words suddenly came out in a rush. "I don't want to leave you on your own, Mum!"

A sigh escaped from her mum. "Oh, Rosa, is that what it is? You mustn't worry about me. You know I'd be so happy if you got into the Royal Ballet School. In a way it would be like a dream come true for me.

Yes, it would mean you boarding and I'd miss you of course, but there are phone calls and emails, and I could come and visit. And you'd be home in the holidays."

"But you said you didn't want me to go away!" Rosa cried.

"I know, however, I had been about to say, but of course I'd cope and I'd be so happy for you – but you'd already left the room." Her mum took her hand. "I do want you to audition, I really do."

Rosa felt as if a massive weight had been

lifted from her shoulders. "Oh wow! Then I will!"

"Why don't we fill in the audition forms right now," said her mum happily.

Rosa nodded and fetched a pen from her bedside table. As she did so, her mum spotted the shell.

"Where did that come from?" she asked. "I've not seen it before."

Rosa hesitated and then smiled. "Oh, someone I know gave it to me." She picked it up. "Can I ring Olivia before we fill in the form? I've got to tell her I'm going to be auditioning after all."

Her mum smiled. "Of course."

Rosa skipped a pace and spun round as she followed her mum out of the bedroom.

She was going to audition for the Royal Ballet School! How amazing was that?

Almost as amazing as having magic ballet shoes, she told herself. *And having brilliant adventures in Enchantia!*

She lifted the shell and smiled to herself as she heard the music of the sea ringing in her ear.

Darcey's Magical Masterclass

Balancés de Côté

This pretty move means 'to sway side to side' in graceful motions. Imagine you are dancing as if you are underwater like Rosa!

1.
Start by sliding your right leg out to 2nd position and push firmly off your left leg, opening up your arms.

2.
Put your weight on to your right leg and bend it slightly, sweeping your left arm into 3rd position and follow the movement with your head so your body is curved softly in the same direction.

3.
Tuck your left foot
behind your right
ankle and put your
weight on to the ball
of your right foot.

4.
Bend your knees and
gently bob down,
hold for one count
and come up straight.
Then start again, but
this time begin with
your left leg. You will
sway in the other
direction!

Magic Ballerina™

Rosa and the Magic Dream

The Wicked Fairy has cast a spell

on Rosa and is holding her captive.

Will she be able to escape?

**Read on for a sneak preview
of book eleven...**

°○·*·☆·○·*·☆·○·*·☆·○·*·°

Rosa heard a faint noise through the trees behind her –
like someone crying out. She spun round. What was it?
"Hello?' she called. But there was no answer.

Then, suddenly, a carriage pulled by two white horses
came around the bend in the track ahead of her. Rosa
expected the carriage to sweep straight past but, to her
surprise, it stopped. The driver jumped down and
opened the carriage door.

Rosa stared as she saw a beautiful lady with long
blonde hair and a pink sparkly dress sitting inside.
"Hello," said the lady smiled. "You must be Rosa."
"Yes, yes I am," Rosa replied.

The lady smiled. "I thought you must be. My name's
Serendipity. I'm a friend of Nutmeg's. "I'm so glad I
found you. Nutmeg can't come to meet you so she
sent me instead. Get into my carriage and we'll go to
my castle."

Rosa hesitated. "Oh, do get in," Serendipity urged. "It's
so cold out." Taking a quick look around her, Rosa got
into the carriage and the driver shut the door with a bang.
As she did so, Rosa was sure she heard a faint cry
of, "Rosa!"

She looked round. "What was that?"

"I didn't hear anything," said Serendipity,
shrugging.

"Someone said my name!"

"Drive on!" Serendipity called to the driver and with
that they sped away…

°ⓖ.*.☆.ⓖ.*.☆.ⓖ.*.☆.ⓖ.*.°

Magic Ballerina™

Darcey Bussell

Buy more great Magic Ballerina books direct from HarperCollins
at 10% off recommended retail price.
FREE postage and packing in the UK.

Delphie and the Magic Ballet Shoes	ISBN 978 0 00 728607 2
Delphie and the Magic Spell	ISBN 978 0 00 728608 9
Delphie and the Masked Ball	ISBN 978 0 00 728610 2
Delphie and the Glass Slippers	ISBN 978 0 00 728617 1
Delphie and the Fairy Godmother	ISBN 978 0 00 728611 9
Delphie and the Birthday Show	ISBN 978 0 00 728612 6
Rosa and the Secret Princess	ISBN 978 0 00 730029 7
Rosa and the Golden Bird	ISBN 978 0 00 730030 3
Rosa and the Magic Moonstone	ISBN 978 0 00 730031 0
Rosa and the Special Prize	ISBN 978 0 00 730032 7
Rosa and the Magic Dream	ISBN 978 0 00 730033 4
Rosa and the Three Wishes	ISBN 978 0 00 730034 1

All priced at £3.99

To purchase by Visa/Mastercard/Switch simply call
08707871724 or fax on **08707871725**

To pay by cheque, send a copy of this form with a cheque made payable to
'HarperCollins Publishers' to: Mail Order Dept. (Ref: BOB4),
HarperCollins Publishers, Westerhill Road, Bishopbriggs, G64 2QT,
making sure to include your full name, postal address and phone number.

From time to time HarperCollins may wish to use your personal data
to send you details of other HarperCollins publications and offers.
If you wish to receive information on other HarperCollins publications
and offers please tick this box ☐

Do not send cash or currency. Prices correct at time of press.
Prices and availability are subject to change without notice.
Delivery overseas and to Ireland incurs a £2 per book postage and packing charge.